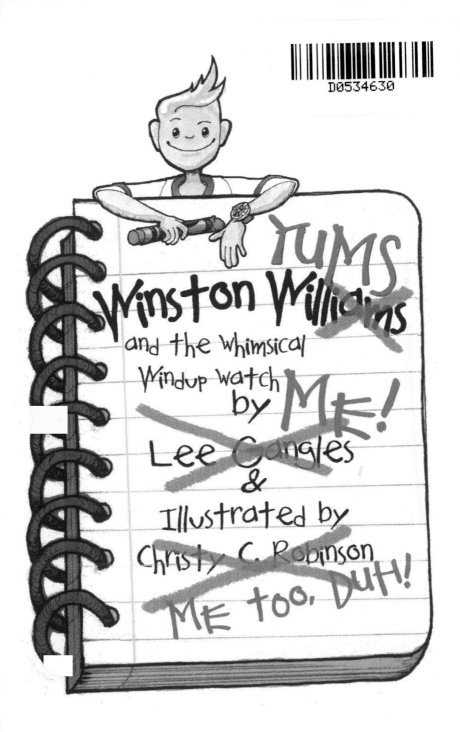

YUMS
~~Winston Williams~~

and the Whimsical Windup Watch

by ~~Lee Gangles~~ **ME!**

&

Illustrated by

~~Christy C. Robinson~~

ME too, DUH!

Contact author, Lee Gangles, in any of the following ways:
On his website at www.leegangles.com
On Facebook at https://www.facebook.com/leeganglesauthor/
By Email at leegangles@leegangles.com
By mail at Lee Gangles, PO Box 9201 Rapid City, SD 57709

Contact the illustrator, Christy C. Robinson, in any of the following ways:
On Facebook at https://www.facebook.com/christycrobinsondesign/
By Email at ccrdesign@gmail.com

Other Works by Lee Gangles: Ferbert Flembuzzle's Most Exotic Zoo

This book is text set in Garamond and Winston Willyums. The artwork for each
picture is an ink drawing rendered with graphic marker.

Paperback ISBN: 978-1-948725-02-6
Ebook ISBN: 978-1-948725-03-3

iii

AUTHOR DEDICATION

To all the kids who see the world differently, don't think the same way as everyone else, or struggle to be understood. I hope you find a whimsical watch of your own so that others (especially grown-ups) can see what you see.

ILLUSTRATOR DEDICATION

To my five little brothers and the good 'ol days when you characters were a whole posse of Winstons.

CONTENTS

1. OLD GEEZERS' HOME

"Looks like trouble just walked through the door!" Lottie said when she saw me step into the old geezers' home.

The old geezers' home is where Pappy lives (he's my dad's dad). Lottie is a lady who works there. She's sturdy. *Sturdy* is the word Mom says I should use to describe people Lottie's size. She says I'm not allowed to say the other word 'cause it is *socially unacceptable*, whatever that means.

1

Lottie's my favorite person at the old geezers' home, other than Pappy and his roommates. So, I guess I should actually say that she's my fourth favorite person but my first favorite out of the people who work there. Everyone else that works there is the worst—especially Mr. Norman.

Mr. Norman runs the old geezers' home, but I guess he's not any good at that job. Pappy says, "Mr. Norman is nothing more than a no-good, plundering, thieving, evil pirate who cares more about taking money from geezers than taking care of geezers."

Dad says Mr. Norman is not an evil pirate and that he is just a *fiscally minded businessman*. Dad always uses a ton of grown-up words that don't make any sense. Sometimes he tries to explain them, but he's usually not very good at explaining in a way I understand.

Anyways, the reason I like Lottie is 'cause she's not like Mr. Norman—she's fun and nice. I also like the way she talks; she always sounds jolly. Pappy says that's the way all *Southern belles* sound. He says a Southern belle is someone who's full of sugars and honeys, which they use to sweeten you up. He also says that, if I'm not careful, a Southern belle my own age will use her sugars and honeys to make me fall in love. I told him I'll never fall in love with anyone, but he says I shouldn't be so sure.

Lottie used her Southern belle voice when she called me trouble. She was just goofing around. It's what we always do. She acts like I'm a troublemaker, and I'll pretend to be tough and mean.

I know Lottie is only pretending 'cause of one time when Dad was with me (which was forever ago, 'cause he never comes to the geezers' home anymore). Me and Lottie were both pretending like I was a real, live troublemaker. Dad got all upset but only with me. I tried to explain how it was all for goofs, but he wouldn't listen.

"Winston, pretending is a child's game, and Lottie

is a grown woman. If she says your trouble, it means you are," he'd said, then he apologized to Lottie. "Please forgive my son's behavior. Sometimes he forgets his manners."

"Honey, no apology necessary. I didn't mean what I said. Just egging the boy on. The blame is mine," Lottie had said to Dad. "Why, Winston is a peach, visiting these lonely folks more than anyone else in town. I think the only reason anyone around here still smiles is because of him."

"That is very kind of you to try and cover for my son's behavior, but it is not necessary." Dad had said, not even believing Lottie. "My boy knows better than to backtalk a grown woman, and he's sorry. Isn't that right, Winston?"

After that me and Lottie agreed that we'd only pretend when I visited without Mom or Dad, which is most of the time. Mom and Dad weren't with me this time, which is why Lottie called me trouble.

"I'll give you trouble, Lottie Dottie," I said back

in my most serious troublemaker voice.

Lottie just laughed super loud. Her whole sturdy body bounces when she laughs.

To act even more serious, I gave Lottie my meanest face, but she just laughed harder, which made me want to smile, so I had to squeeze my lips super-duper tight.

"Sugar, you're too late to give me trouble. Your grandpappy and those two stooges he shares a room with made me immune to trouble." She gave me a wink as she slid a Yum-Yum Chocolate Bar across the counter. "Now, honey, you best sign in and hurry on back."

I finally smiled, 'cause Yum-Yum Chocolate Bars are my favorite, and then I ran to Pappy's room.

Pappy and his roommates, Tick and Tock, all cheered when I entered. Tick pretended to play a trumpet while Tock called out, "Introducing Winston the Great!"

I tried to walk like a king, but only for a few steps,

before running and giving Pappy a huge hug. Pappy is skinny and old. I don't know how old, but I think he's super old 'cause he has a cane and white hair—completely white.

Tick and Tock are brothers. They're also old, but they only have gray hair, so they aren't *as* old as Pappy—I think. Tick's gray hair is on the top of his head, but Tock's head is shiny and bald. Luckily, I can still tell he's old, 'cause he has gray hair in his goatee. Both of 'em are shorter and sturdier than Pappy.

I don't know their real names, but Tick and Tock

is what I've always called 'em. The reason is that if you ever ask them how they're doing, they say the same thing every time.

"Just waiting for the end," Tock will say with a wink, and then they'll go back and forth like they are pretending to be a clock.

Tick always says, "Tick."

Tock always says, "Tock."

"Tick."

"Tock."

"Tick."

"Tock."

I'm not sure what *end* they are waiting for, but I do know that they love clocks, which is why they like the names I gave 'em better than their real names.

"Shame we didn't get such great nicknames 'til we were old geezers," they'd told me. "We could have used names like those back when we owned our clock and watch repair shop."

Pappy says the nicknames I chose are perfect for

a couple of old dogs. Of course, Dad, who's a boring lawyer, says that nicknaming the elderly is not respectful.

"Come now, Winston," Pappy said with a huge grin. "Tell us what great adventures you've had."

I thought for a moment and shrugged. "No adventures. I just got yelled at a lot."

"What do you mean no adventures? Yelling is one of the hallmarks of adventure." Pappy slapped his knee. "I hope you're keeping notes in your adventure log."

My *adventure log* is a notebook that Pappy gave me so I could write down all the cool stuff that happens. Pappy says it's important to put your adventures on paper 'cause the older you get the harder it is to remember them.

Tick and Tock say that forgetting your adventures is one of the worst things that can happen to someone. They say that forgetting adventures will ruin the most heroic heroes.

I don't want to be lame or boring, so I keep an adventure log, but I don't exactly write much in it. I mostly draw pictures and only make small notes.

"Now, don't leave us hanging. Tell us everything." Pappy leaned forward.

"Well . . ." I thought for a moment. "Ms. Perkles yelled at me and sent me to the principal; a bus driver yelled at me for something I didn't even do; and Mom yelled at me for making dinner. That's when the school called, and Mom sent me over here so she and Dad can *figure out what to do about my behavior.*" I shrugged. "Nothing else, I guess."

"Hot dog," Tick said. "That there is a whole heap of adventures."

"Only problem is that you started at the end," Tock added. "Back those tales up."

"Indeed," Pappy said. "You don't pull a train with the caboose. Start from the beginning. Why'd ya get sent to the principal?"

"Tell us more about the bus driver," said Tick.

"And I wanna hear more about that infamous dinner," said Tock.

"Well," I mumbled, "there's not much to tell."

"Hold on," Pappy interrupted. "That's no way to start an adventure. Start with a touch of hugger-mugger."

"Hugger-mugger?" I asked.

"You don't know hugger-mugger? What are schools teaching these days?" Tick asked.

"Hugger-mugger! Intrigue! Mystery!" Tock said. "Something to get people on the edge of their seats, you know, a hook, something to draw us in.'"

"But Dad says you should always start with the facts and stick to the facts," I told them. "He says people don't have time for anything but the facts."

"PFFFFFFFFFFFFFFT." Pappy stuck out his tongue and blew raspberries—a lot of raspberries. "The only thing Henry knows about storytelling is how to suck all the fun out of it."

Henry's my dad, and Pappy is his dad, which is

why he calls him Henry.

"So, I shouldn't listen to Dad?"

"Uh, well. . ." Pappy looked nervous. "You should listen to him on all the other stuff, just not storytelling. That boy never kept an adventure log like I told him to, so he never learned the proper art."

Pappy was right. Dad is bad at telling stories. Sometimes, at dinner, he'll tell Mom about what happened at his boring lawyer job. They are the worst stories ever, and I mean the worst. So boring!

"Now, forget everything Henry told you about how to ruin stories," Pappy continued, "and tell the adventures the way you want them to be remembered."

So, I did, starting with Ms. Perkles.

2. HyPeR-BULLiES

W-i-n-s-t-o-n W-i-l-l-... . . .

Ms. Perkles hovered over me like a giant gargoyle while I wrote my name. She always does that when she wants to start arguments about the way my name is spelled.

Once, I told Dad about Ms. Perkles always starting fights. He didn't look up; he just told me he didn't have time to listen to my hyper-bullies.

"Yes!" I told him. "That's exactly what she is: a

bully—a hyper-bully—just like you said."

"That's not what I said." Dad rubbed his temples and shook his head. "It's hyperbole, not hyper-bully." Then he sounded it out really slow: "*Hi-per-bo-lee*. In other words, I don't have time for your embellishments." I gave him the look that says he wasn't making any sense. He sighed. "Hyperbole is just another way of saying you're telling a tall tale, stretching the truth, exaggerating, making things sound worse than they really are. Just do whatever Ms. Perkles says and no more hyperboles."

"What if she tells me to rob a bank?" I asked, but Dad didn't answer. He just shook his head again and went back to typing on the computer.

Anyway, I knew Ms. Perkles was about to start a fight again, but I didn't care. I finished writing my name the way it is supposed to be spelled.

W-i-l-l-y-u-m-s

Ms. Perkles cleared her throat. "Winston, we've been through this far too many times. You know that's not how you spell Williams."

"Ugggggh," I sighed.

Ms. Perkles hates it when I ugh—she says it is the most disrespectful noise I could make, but Mom says farting and burping really loud on purpose are the most disrespectful noises.

I explained to Ms. Perkles that I only ugh'd because I wanted her to know she wasn't being as smart as a teacher should be. Most of the time when I ugh, Ms. Perkles will only lecture me—sometimes I even lose recess—but she looked extra mad this time.

"Winston, you know it's spelled W-i-l-l-*i-a-m-s*. We've been through this at least a hundred times."

We hadn't been through it a hundred times. "If I spelled it your way, it wouldn't make any sense," I told her. "Just listen to the sounds. Will-*yums*! Will-*yums*! Trust me, I know how to spell yum." I knew 'cause of Yum-Yum Chocolate Bars.

"Excuse me?" Ms. Perkles said. She was using

the same type of voice Mom does when she is acting surprised but is actually mad, which is confusing. "I'm not sure I like your tone," she said.

I had to think quick, so I said something Dad says a lot. "I have principals, and I will stick to them."

Whenever Dad says it, Mom always says how proud she is to be married to a man with principals, which is confusing. The only place I know with principals is a school, and Dad isn't even in school anymore. Also, schools only have one principal, so even if Dad was still in school, I didn't know how he could have more than one. Even though it doesn't make any sense, Mom is always proud of him for it. The weird thing was that even though I had a principal, Ms. Perkles wasn't proud of me.

"What are you even talking about?" she asked, suddenly looking more confused than mad.

I explained about Dad sticking to his principals, even though he's not in school anymore and how Mom is always proud of him. When I was done, I told her how it was time for her to be proud of me, like Mom, for sticking to my principals.

Ms. Perkles made a face I didn't understand and shook her head. "It's princi*ples* not princi*pals*." I think she realized she wasn't making any sense 'cause then she said, "A princi*ple* is a value, like being honest. It's not the same as a school principal."

"Uhh . . . right. Principle is what I meant to—"

"But since you are so keen on sticking to your princi*pals*—" Ms. Perkles interrupted me.

I guess she didn't realize she interrupted me, so I stopped her to let her know. "Lady"—she always calls the girls in the class *young ladies*, but Ms. Perkles is not very young, so I just said the lady part—"you interrupted me, which is breaking a class rule. You said so yourself."

Ms. Perkles raised her eyebrows, and her eyes got super wide. She looked like a cartoon who was about to have steam shoot out of her ears. That's when I remembered one of the rules she made special, just for me: no calling her *lady*.

She took a big, loud breath. "What I was about to say before *you* so rudely interrupted *me* was that, since you are so keen on principals, you can march yourself down to the principal's office right now."

I know she didn't actually mean for me to march, but I like marching, so I swung my arms like a soldier and raised my knees high with each step. All the way to the principal's office I called out, "Hup, two, hup, two."

I didn't even have to ask for directions, like most kids. I know right where the principal's office is. I've been there a bunch of times. Mom says that's nothing to be proud of, which is confusing 'cause she's always proud of Dad when he can get somewhere without asking for directions.

The waiting room outside Mr. L's office has soft chairs to sit in while you wait, which is a good thing, 'cause Mr. L (he's the principal) is never ready when I get there. I waited a loooong time, before he finally was.

"Mr. Lazzidonowicks will see you now," Mrs. Butters told me.

Mrs. Butters is Mr. L's recept-a-something-or-other. I can't remember the word, but I know she is not his secretary—she was very clear about that. Basically, she guards Mr. L's door. I think she got the job 'cause she's the only person I know who can say Mr. L's actual name.

"Winston, take a seat," Mr. L told me when I walked in. "I was really hoping we wouldn't have to have another one of these talks."

"You don't want to talk to me?" I asked. Before

he answered, I explained how extremely rude it is to tell someone that you don't want to talk to them— at least that's what Mom tells me.

"That's not exactly what I meant." Mr. L made a weird smile. Then he started saying a bunch of other stuff. He's like Dad, always using words I don't understand, so listening is really hard, even when I try my best. When Mr. L was all done, he asked me if I understood.

"Uh, yeah," I told him, even though that wasn't exactly true, but I had a good reason for not being exactly true. Asking if I understand is a trick, I think. If I tell him no, he just says, "Let me try explaining it this way," and then says everything all over again, the exact same way, with the exact same big words.

After I figured out his trick, I just always say that I understand.

"Great! Since you've learned your lesson, no need to call your parents this time, but if it happens again, your mother and father will need to be at our next meeting." Then he sent me back to class

The bell for the end of school rang right when I got back, so I hurried and grabbed my backpack and left before Ms. Perkles could start any more arguments.

3. FrANkLiN

There are two ways home. One way I don't take 'cause of the haunted zombie house you have to pass. It's this old, scary house that has boards nailed over the windows and peeling paint. It's dark inside and creepy on the outside. I know it's a zombie house because Max (he's my friend) told me so.

He said that his older brother said that zombies live in the house and that, if you get too close, the zombies will jump out of the windows and eat your brains. He also said zombies can't be killed because they aren't actually alive—they're something called *undead*, which I guess means they aren't alive or dead. I don't really understand it.

What I do know is that after Max told me about zombies, I had nightmares for a week where zombies chased me and tried to eat my brains. Mom says there's no such thing as zombies, but I'm not sure how much moms know about that kind of stuff.

Dad says there is no such thing as haunted houses. He said the house is only *condemned*, which he said means it's *uninhabitable*. I didn't understand either of those words. When I asked what *uninhabitable* meant, he rolled his eyes, which I didn't appreciate, 'cause he was the one not making any sense. "It's when a house is so run down that no one can live in it," he said.

"What about things that aren't alive, like the undead?" I asked. "Like zombies?"

He didn't answer my question. "Winston, aren't

you a little too old to believe in zombies?" he asked. "The real problem with a condemned structure is what it does to the property values of nearby homes."

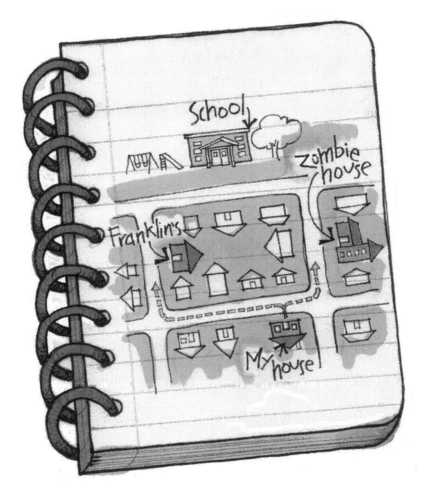

I'm not afraid of property values (maybe 'cause I don't know what they are), but I am still afraid of zombies. That's why I don't go home the haunted zombie house way.

The other way isn't haunted and doesn't have zombies, but it has other problems. For one, it's longer, but the worst problem is Franklin. He's a big, mean, fart-faced, booger-brained, ugly, smelly, snot-drooling bully who picks on me. But he's never tried to eat my brains, so I'm less afraid of him than zombies.

Franklin's a fifth grader, or at least he would be a fifth grader if he went to school. He went to school last year, but now he's homeschooled. Max said Franklin got expelled, which means he was kicked out. Max said it was 'cause he dunked a kindergartner's head in the toilet and flushed it, which is called a swirly.

Mom says I shouldn't worry about why Franklin's parents chose to homeschool him. Dad says I shouldn't listen to rumors unless they're backed by evidence and that I should mind my own business.

I try to mind my own business. It's Franklin who doesn't mind his, unless his business is being a bully. He bullies me every time he sees me. One time, he took my backpack and dumped everything on the ground. Another time, he told me he wouldn't let me pass until I jumped on one foot 100 times. When I got to 57, he said he was bored, pushed me over, and went inside.

Another time, he made me yell as loudly as I could that I was the dumbest kid in the world, which is a lie. I yelled it—but only because he told me that if I didn't, he was going to give me an atomic wedgie. If you don't know what an atomic wedgie is, you should know it is worse than lying.

I really hoped Franklin wouldn't be outside, but he was. I saw him standing on the sidewalk, waiting for me. I pretended I didn't see him and crossed to the other side of the street.

"Hey, Whiny-baby-ston!" he yelled. That's what he calls me 'cause he says I'm whiny, and I'm a baby, and my name is dumb. In his words, "When you add all those together, you get Whiny-baby-ston." Obviously, he isn't learning math at homeschool, 'cause you add numbers, not words.

I pretended I couldn't hear him.

"Hey!" he yelled again. "I know you heard me!"

I kept looking at the ground and started walking faster. Then Franklin threw a huge clump of mud that hit me on the shoulder and splattered all over the side of my face.

"Yeah, you!" Franklin yelled. "I'm talking to you! Come over here right now, or I'll drag you over and shove your face in the mud!" I didn't want my face in the mud, so I went over. "You're a bad listener," he said, and then he spit on the ground right by my feet.

I don't like Franklin, but I have to admit, he is pretty good at spitting. Whenever I try, I get spit all over my chin.

I didn't say anything at first, so he put me in a headlock. "Say you're sorry, or I'll make you sorry." That just means he is going to push me, punch me, or take something from me. I didn't want any of those things.

"I'm sorry," I told him, but I didn't mean it.

"Good." He let go of me. "Put out your hands!"

"Why?"

"Just do it!"

I put my hands out. Franklin reached down and scooped up a big handful of mud, and then he dumped it in my hands.

"What'd ya do that for?" I asked.

He laughed. "Now slap yourself in the face!"

"No way!"

"DO IT!" Franklin made a fist.

I got ready to slap myself, but before I did, Franklin stopped me.

"Wait. I got a better idea," he told me.

He was looking at something behind me. I turned around. A big, yellow school bus was coming up the road.

"Throw the mud at the bus," he ordered me.

I shook my head, 'cause I'd rather slap myself in the face. Throwing stuff at the bus will get you in super huge, gigantic trouble—we had a whole school assembly all about it.

"Do it, or you'll be double sorry."

He'd never threatened me with being double sorry, and I didn't want to find out what that meant.

"Fine."

"Launch in five, four, three, two—" Franklin suddenly stopped the countdown and put his muddy hands behind his back.

The bus driver slammed on the brakes and stopped the bus right next to us. The door flew open, and Ms. Kratz, the bus driver, stared at me.

Ms. Kratz is an older lady—not like old geezer old, but still older. She has crooked teeth that are all yellow, and her black hair sticks out like she's been electrocuted. She is the scariest lady I know. Scarier than Franklin, but still not as scary as zombies.

"Think it's funny to throw mud at my bus?" she asked.

"But . . . but I didn't—"

She didn't let me finish telling the true story.

"Yet! You didn't yet. Is that what you were gonna say?" She shook her head with her nostrils all flared open which made it so I could see dried boogers in her nose. "I saw you standing there with your arm pulled back, ready to throw that mud. You think it's funny to make me stay late, cleaning mud off my bus? Well, do you?"

"No. I—"

Franklin, still holding his muddy hands behind his back, cut me off. "Ms. Kratz, I tried to stop Winston, but he just threatened to slap me in the face with all that mud. He told me he was gonna throw the mud at your bus and blame it on me."

Franklin looked at me and shook his head before adding, "Tried stopping him, but he wouldn't listen."

"Thank you, young man." She smiled at Franklin. "As for you"—she stopped smiling and looked back at me—"give me your full name and grade. Your teacher will be hearing about this."

After she drove away, Franklin gave me a stupid grin and still made me slap myself in the face.

As he walked back into his house, I yelled, "One of these days, you're gonna be so afraid of me, you'll pee your pants."

Franklin laughed, like he thought I was joking, but I wasn't.

4. THE WORST BABYSITTER

When I got home, Val's car was in the driveway. Val is my cousin. She's sixteen. On the days that Mom is working, Val's *supposed* to babysit me, but she is the worst babysitter ever! All she does is watch TV and play on her phone.

One time, I told Dad what a bad babysitter she is and how she doesn't pay any attention to me. Dad just said, "We're not paying her to be your friend. If the house is still standing when I get home, I'm happy."

Mom always says we should consider ourselves lucky Val is willing to take the job and that it's *hard to find an affordable babysitter who's willing to tolerate my disposition.* I asked what that meant, but she wouldn't say.

I told Mom to just quit her job, so they wouldn't need Val to watch me. She told me she needs her job because of how expensive it is to raise me, which doesn't make any sense. I don't charge Mom or Dad any money, so how could I be expensive?

The only good part about Val babysitting is that most of the time she lets me watch TV, as long as I don't ask too many questions. That's what I was gonna do after getting bullied by Franklin—watch TV—but Val wouldn't even let me sit down.

"Ewwww! You're all"—Val stuck out her tongue and made a face like she just ate a disgusting bug—"gross. Stay away from the couch."

"You can't tell me what to do. You don't even live here, so you don't get to make the rules."

"Uh, yeah, I kinda do. Your mom and dad basically pay me to be the boss of you." She smiled, but it wasn't a nice one. It was more like she thought she was soooo cool, even though she's not. "How'd you get so filthy, anyway?" she asked.

"I don't want to talk about it."

"Fine, be a twerp, but you're not allowed in this room until you're not a disgusting mud monster."

I stuck my tongue out at Val, which Mom says is a childish thing to do, but Val did the exact thing back and ordered me to go wash. I didn't like being ordered around by someone that does childish things.

I also didn't want to leave because she was watching this show where guys were playing baseball with fruit instead of a ball. It was awesome 'cause every time they hit the fruit with the bat, it exploded into a bunch of pieces. I told Val I would just stand, but she wouldn't even let me do that.

Not wanting to miss any of the fruit baseball, I ran to the bathroom to wash as fast as a I could. When I got back, Val had changed the channel to some dumb cooking show.

"Not fair. Go back to the guys exploding fruit!" I told her.

"Beggars don't get to be choosers." She shrugged.

"What does that even mean?" I asked.

She just ugh'd and rolled her eyes. "It means I get to choose the channel, and you don't."

I tried telling Val how unfair that was, but she interrupted me.

"You watch with your eyes, not your mouth."

"Duh," I told her. "I'm not stupid. I know how to watch TV."

Mom doesn't like when I say *stupid*. She says it's a bad word, but Val says it a lot.

"Obviously you are stupid, or you'd have shut

your face by now."

"That's impossible," I explained. "Faces don't shut."

She gave me a weird look, and then her mouth dropped open like she didn't believe me.

"It's true," I told her. "I'm surprised you didn't know that."

"Holy . . . cow . . ." Val rolled her eyes, again. "It means stop talking. You take everything way too literal."

One time, Dad told me the same thing—not about shutting my face but about taking things too literal. I made the mistake of asking what literal meant.

(WARNING! Confusing, lawyer definition is coming up. If you don't understand any of it, that's GOOD! It means you're **not** a lame, boring, grown-up.)

He said, "Literal is when you accept things at face

value instead of applying the latent and metaphoric contexts in order to understand the true meaning of what someone is saying."

Since I'm not a boring lawyer, I had no idea what any of that meant. I only knew it made absolutely zero sense. I also think some of those words might have been another language.

I'd decided I didn't care what *literal* meant. I figured it was obviously something only grown-ups knew, but somehow Val knew the word. 'Course she could've just been acting like she knew.

Even though the cooking show wasn't as good as the fruit baseball, I did like that the chef had a funny way of talking. It wasn't like how Lottie talks. This guy was harder to understand. Like, instead of saying "that" and "this," he would say "zat" and "zis." He also talked a lot about what he learned as a young boy in France.

Near the end of the show, he tasted his soup and said, "No, no, no. Eet eez missing za most important ingredients." He cut up some stuff he called basil (but it just looked like a bunch of normal old leaves) and threw it in the pot; then he added salt and pepper and tasted it again. "Ahh-ha. Wee, wee. No dish is complete vithout fresh herbs from za garden and a dash of za salt and pepper."

Watching the chef made me really hungry, so I told Val that I needed a snack.

The first time she didn't say anything. I said it again, but I cleared my throat, like Ms. Perkles does when she wants me to pay attention.

"So what?" Val's eyes stayed stuck on her phone. "Not my problem."

"But you're the babysitter—you're supposed to help me with that stuff."

"Your legs broken?"

"No. Why would that matter? I don't eat with my legs."

"Your arms work?"

"Duh. Can you stop asking dumb questions and

please get me a snack?"

"Well, if your arms and legs aren't broken, walk yourself to the kitchen and figure it out." She finally looked up from her phone. "You can't do anything on your own, can you? So helpless."

After that I didn't even want Val's help anymore. I went to the kitchen and looked for a snack, but my brain was distracted, thinking about how Val said I was helpless, which is completely wrong. I can do lots of things that she can't. Like, if I was a babysitter, I could help make all kinds of food, even a whole dinner.

That's when I decided to prove I wasn't helpless, by making dinner all by myself. If Mom knew I could make dinner, unlike Val, maybe she'd fire Val and let me stay home without a babysitter.

I grabbed a pot and filled it with hot water from the sink, then I put it on the counter. I'm not allowed to use the stove 'cause of possibly burning myself. I remembered that in the chef's soup, there were potatoes, carrots, and chicken. Since carrots are gross, I decided it was best to leave those out.

I'm also not allowed to use knives 'cause of possibly cutting myself, so I needed another way to chop the potatoes. I thought and thought and thought as hard as I could for ways to chop without a knife.

At first, I couldn't think of any ideas, but suddenly, I remembered the guys exploding fruit with a baseball bat, which gave me the best idea.

I ran and grabbed my baseball bat from my room. When I got back to the kitchen, I tossed the potatoes in the air and tried hitting them with the bat, just like on the show. My first swings kept missing, but then I hit a homerun.

The only problems were that the potato didn't explode, and kitchens aren't big enough for homeruns. The potato just bounced off the cabinets, knocked over a bunch of stuff on the counter, and made a ton of noise.

That's when Val yelled, "You better not be making a mess in there!" Of course, she didn't come check 'cause that would mean putting her phone down.

After that, I put the potatoes on the floor and hit 'em like a hammer, which worked perfect and was lots quieter. Plus, all the potato chunks were easy-peasy to scoop up with the dustpan and dump right into the pot.

Next, I got the chicken. For that part I used chicken nuggets 'cause chicken nuggets are my favorite kind of chicken. Mom always keeps a big bag of nuggets in the freezer. Since they're already small, I didn't even have to smash them with my bat.

I stirred it all up and took a sip, like the chef did in the show. It didn't taste so good. The water wasn't hot anymore. The outside part of the chicken nuggets, which is usually crunchy, had washed off and was all mushy. The middle part was still frozen. Also, the potato pieces, which were supposed to be soft, were still crunchy like an apple. I was trying to figure out how to make the soup better when I remembered what the chef said after he tasted his soup.

"No, no, no. Eet eez missing za most important ingredients," I imitated.

No wonder it wasn't any good yet. I forgot spices. I opened the spice cupboard and found salt, but I couldn't find any pepper. I looked everywhere. The normal pepper was lost. The only type of pepper I could find was in the fridge. It was a bottle of

Burnin' Bubba's Bum Blistering Pepper Sauce. Underneath that it said, "Packed with Punch—15 of the Most Potent Peppers Known to Man!" It also said something about how you should never use more than one drop.

I only knew about one kind of pepper—normal pepper. If Burnin' Bubba's had 15 kinds, I figured that one of them had to be normal pepper.

I sprinkled in a tiny bit of salt and one drop of Burnin' Bubba's Bum Blistering Pepper Sauce, mixed it all up again, and did a second taste test.

The parts that were supposed to be crunchy, were still mushy, and the parts that were supposed to be soft were still crunchy, and the chicken was still frozen.

Another problem was that it was also spicy, at least to me. I had to drink two whole glasses of cold milk to make my tongue stop burning. BUT it did taste a tiny bit better

Of course, if I was gonna get Val fired, I didn't

need a tiny bit better. I needed *a lot* better. That's when I decided that if a little salt and one drop of pepper sauce made the soup a little better, a *lot* of salt and a *lot* of drops would obviously make it a *lot* better!

I dumped in all the salt and the whole bottle of Burnin' Bubba's Bum Blistering Pepper Sauce. (I kind of forgot how the bottle said you should never use more than one drop).

I was gonna do another taste, but I heard the garage door open, which meant Mom was home, so there was no time for more taste tests. As fast as I could, I filled bowls, set the table, and waited for her to come in.

When she saw the table, Mom asked, "What's going on here?" She was smiling.

"I made dinner," I said.

"Well, look at you, becoming all responsible." Mom winked. I handed her a bowl of my soup, and she smelled it. "Winston, it smells great,"—she scooped up a spoonful and looked at it—"but it looks . . ." She stopped smiling and started looking all concerned. "What exactly is in this?"

"Only the best ingredients—potatoes, chicken nuggets, and lots of spices!"

I waited for her to take a bite. As soon as she did, she spit it out and coughed a bunch. She opened her mouth like it was on fire and ran to the sink. She didn't use a cup; she just stuck her whole head under and drank straight from the faucet, even though she has told me a bunch of times that I'm not allowed to do that. She stayed there for a long time.

Finally, she said, "What kind of spices?"

I showed her the empty saltshaker and the empty bottle of Burnin' Bubba's Bum Blistering Pepper Sauce. She didn't look like she was proud of me anymore.

"I think I'll just order a pizza," she said as she dumped her bowl into the sink.

I was about to tell her how rude it is to not eat

what I made, 'cause that's what she always tells me when I don't want to eat her food, but I didn't get the chance. Her phone rang.

"Hello, this is Susan . . . Oh yes, Ms. Perkles, how are you?" Mom listened for a bit and then gave me a weird look. "He did what? . . . I would have sent him to the principal, as well . . . Uh huh . . . Oh dear, there's more?"

Mom's weird face changed to her upset face. "He was about to throw what at the bus? Poor, Ms. Kratz. I'm terribly sorry . . . Yes, you and Ms. Kratz deserve far more respect. Thank you for the phone call . . . Yes, you have a wonderful evening, as well."

Mom hung up the phone and asked, "Any idea what that call was about?"

"Maybe." I shrugged. "But it wasn't my faul—"

Mom didn't let me finish. "You're gonna spend the evening with your grandpappy while your father and I figure out what to do about your behavior."

5. MAgIC WatCH

When I got done telling Pappy, Tick, and Tock about all my adventures and showing them my drawings, Pappy slapped his knee. "I sure wish I could still have adventures like those."

"Agreed, agreed," said Tick and Tock at the same time.

Just then, Mr. Norman walked into the room. He is medium height and has a big bushy mustache. He combs the hair from the side of his head over the top where there is no hair. Pappy told me that's called a *comb-over*. He says it's supposed to hide his baldness. I told Pappy that Mr. Norman must not be good at comb-overs, 'cause I can still see almost all his baldness. Pappy chuckled and said Mr. Norman is even worse at running the old geezers' home.

Mr. Norman is fa—I mean sturdy, but he's not sturdy everywhere—just in his belly, which is so sturdy it hangs over his belt buckle. Everywhere else, like his legs, arms, shoulders—all skinny.

Tick and Tock always say Mr. Norman is *one big mess*. I think they're talking about how his shirts are always wrinkly and have weird, yellow stains in the armpits.

Anyway, Mr. Norman walked in and claimed he was there to inspect the room. Pappy told me once that *inspecting the room* is Mr. Norman's way of sticking his nose where it doesn't belong.

"You three are the biggest culprits of energy waste in this facility," Mr. Norman said as he turned off all the lights and unplugged the fans. "You're not paying enough to justify bloated utility bills stemming from running fans and lights all day."

When all the lights were off, it was dark enough that Mr. Norman had to pull out a flashlight to continue his inspection. He peeked behind the dressers, in the bathroom, and under the cushions of the chairs. Then he got down on his hands and knees to look under the beds. That's when Pappy gave Tick and Tock a look that Dad calls a *consciousness of guilt.*

I'd made the mistake of asking what that meant.

(WARNING! Another confusing, boring lawyer definition is coming up. Remember it's GOOD if it doesn't make sense!)

Dad told me, "It is when you express through action, word, or deed a knowledge of your own malcontent and wrongdoing."

Luckily, Mom was there. She's better at

explaining big words. She said, "It's when someone looks guilty because they know they broke a rule."

Well, that's the look Pappy, Tick, and Tock gave each other, but they were also kinda smiling, like they thought something funny was about to happen.

A second later, Mr. Norman started yelling all the bad words I'm not allowed to repeat and some bad words I'd never heard before. I knew they were bad 'cause of the way he said them. He said even more bad words when he bonked his head while crawling out from under the bed.

When he was done, he started yelling at Pappy, Tick, and Tock. "I've told you a dozen times I will not allow you to turn this room into a massive fire hazard! No packing the underside of your bed with flammables!" He looked like he was throwing a grown-up temper tantrum. "Consider this your final warning. Clean it out before the end of the week, or I'll confiscate and dispose of all of it myself . . . at your expense, of course."

"Where do you expect us to put all of our treasures?" Pappy asked.

Mr. Norman pointed toward some tiny shelves on the wall—one near each bed. Pappy's shelf was full, but all it was holding was six books. Tick and Tock had a small clock on each of their shelves—cuckoo clocks.

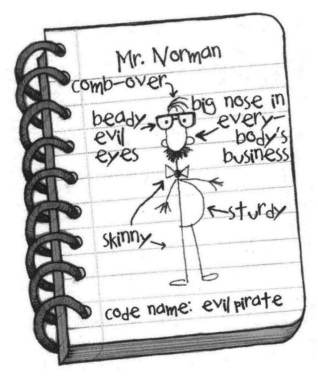

Tick's cuckoo clock is a normal one with a bird

that pops out of it. It's the first clock he ever got.

Tock's cuckoo clock is my favorite. Instead of a bird, it has a little wooden donkey and a little wooden farmer. They look like mini puppets—the kind that usually have strings, but these don't. Every hour, the farmer moves over to the donkey and then the donkey kicks with his back legs, knocking the farmer into a small barrel. Actual bubbles start floating out of the barrel, as if the farmer is blowing bubbles under water. Then, the donkey *hee-haws* the same number as the time of day.

"I've provided you—" As Mr. Norman was talking, it turned six o'clock, and Tock's cuckoo clock started.

Hee-haw!

Mr. Norman's face tightened. "Provided you ample—"

Hee-haw!

His eyes got bigger. "Ample space to—"

Hee-haw!

". . . to store your—"

Hee-haw!

Mr. Norman turned red like a tomato and raised his voice. "Your junk!"

Hee-haw!

He scrunched his eyes and made fists. "Is that clock quite—"

Hee-haw!

Mr. Norman stopped talking and waited until he knew for sure the clock was done. We were all laughing—well, everyone but Mr. Norman. He looked super mad, which is why I was trying to hide my laughs behind my hands. Pappy, Tick, and Tock didn't hide their laughs at all.

"You think that's funny?" Mr. Norman marched over to the shelf and got so close to the clock that he had to lift up his glasses. "We'll see if you think it is still funny once I disable this ridiculous donkey clock."

That's when the clock on Tick's shelf turned six

o'clock. A bird on the end of a spring shot out, and I guess Mr. Norman was standing too close, 'cause his face kind of got in the way, and the bird's beak jabbed him right in the eye.

Mr. Norman covered his eye with his hand and yelled more bad words.

"That clock always did run a little slow." Tick laughed. Mr. Norman did not.

"Everything better be gone by the end of the week!" Mr. Norman shouted as he stomped out of the room.

I asked Pappy why Mr. Norman was so mad about the beds, and Pappy told me to look underneath. It was completely full of books. Under Tick and Tock's beds was nothing but old clocks and watches.

"Mr. Norman is always saying that if we don't get rid of our treasures, he is going to take 'em, like a scoundrel pirate," Tock told me as he started turning the lights back on and plugging the fans back in.

"He's been threatening that for over a year, but he's never followed through," Tick added.

"He doesn't have the right to take our treasures," said Pappy.

"Why don't you just move to a different geezers' home?" I asked.

"Wish I could," Pappy said, "but Henry won't allow it. He stuck me in here, and he doesn't even visit me anymore."

"We've both got kids just like Henry—forcing us to be here and never visiting," Tock said.

I couldn't tell if Pappy, Tick, and Tock were sad or mad, but I think I understood how they felt. Mom and Dad send me to my room a lot, which makes me mad. Sometimes I am there so long that I start to think they forgot about me, which always makes me sad. If Mom and Dad forgot about me for real, I bet I'd be super sad.

"But you're more grown up than Dad, so can't you leave whenever you want?" I asked.

"Nope." Pappy frowned. "Henry used his lawyer voodoo to convince a judge that I am too old to make my own decisions. Now he gets to choose everything as if I'm *his* kid."

"No fair!" I said. "You're older. You should be bossing him around."

"Eh,"—Pappy waved his hand—"nobody should ever boss anyone else around."

"Wish I could help, but I'm just a kid. Grown-ups don't listen to me."

"Nonsense." Pappy gave me a hug, and then he smiled. "We're old and we've lived long lives. It's us who should be helping you."

"But I don't have to live in a geezers' home. What do I need help with?"

"All those adventures of yours, that's what. It's a crying shame that Ms. Perkles, that bully, and Val don't believe you." Pappy frowned for a moment, but then he smiled. "But now that I'm putting my brain to it, I think Tick and Tock have something,

55

uh . . . whimsical they might want to give you—something that might solve your problems."

Tick and Tock looked at Pappy all funny, like they didn't understand. Then they looked at each other, still confused. All the sudden, they got really excited, like they both just had the same great idea as Pappy. Tick jumped up and got something from his nightstand: an old, rotten looking sock.

I didn't want a smelly old sock! Which is what I was about to tell Tick, but then he dumped something out of the sock, into his hand. He held it up with a grin. It was a watch.

It was the strangest watch I'd ever seen. It wasn't digital, like I was hoping. It was like the old clocks on their shelves, with a minute hand and an hour hand that pointed to the numbers, only this watch had lots of pointers and dials. The numbers looked like they had gotten stuck in a tornado and now they were all confused.

The 1 was bigger than all the other numbers and

in its normal spot—well, it was sort of in its normal spot. The rest of the numbers got smaller and were all mixed up in a spiral, like water going down a drain. It looked almost like one of those wheels they use to hypnotize people.

I put it on as tight as it would go, but it was still way too big. It dangled on my wrist like one of Mom's bracelets. Tick said not to worry and that by morning it would fit perfect. I gave him my I-don't-believe-you look, but he just said to wait and see.

"Thanks," I said. Even though it didn't fit, I still thought it was pretty cool. "Of course, I only know how to tell time on a digital watch."

"Don't go worrying about that," said Tick. "You'll figure that out eventually. For now, you just need to follow our instructions very carefully. If you do, the watch does way more than just tell time."

"Seriously?" I asked. "Does it have a calculator— a stopwatch? 'Cause I have friends with watches that do those things, which I think is awesome, even though Dad says a watch is only for telling time and nothin' else."

"No, no calculator or stopwatch," Tock explained. "In fact, this watch doesn't even have a battery. It's windup."

"Then what's so special 'bout it?" I was feeling less excited and a little bummed.

"That part you will have to wait to see," said Tick. "Let's just say it helps others understand you a little better—like a very special lucky charm."

"But like we said, there's instructions," Tock said.

I like lucky charms. I have a lucky rabbit's foot, lucky pennies, and even a four-leaf clover, but none of those come with rules. They're just automatically lucky. I wasn't sure I wanted a lucky charm with instructions, but I listened, anyway.

Tick and Tock said the first step was to wind it up. They showed me how to spin the outer part of the watch counterclockwise. As I spun it, the numbers spiraled in reverse and moved to where they were supposed to be.

"Once you wind it, it'll automatically set to the correct time," Tock said.

The hands started spinning on their own until the short hand pointed at the 6 and the long hand pointed at the 1.

"Awesome," I said. "Is that the special part?"

Tick and Tock giggled and shook their heads.

"No, the special part is waaaay more special," Tick said.

"How so?"

Tock frowned. "Like we said, we can't really explain it. Gotta experience it."

"The only downside is that the specialness won't last forever—only one day—and then you'll have to wind the watch up again and start all over."

"Besides winding it up," said Tick, "all you gotta do is say the magic phrase."

"The magic phrase?" I was getting confused and worried and a little annoyed. I wouldn't remember all these rules. Also, I started thinking that maybe Tick and Tock were just playing a big joke. "What's the magic phrase?"

"I don't know," said Tock. "It's different for everyone. The words only come to your mind when you really, truly, honestly need them."

That part really sounded made up. That's why I started asking the tough questions.

"If this watch is so special, why would you give it to me?"

Tick and Tock both frowned and Tick said, "I think we're too old. It stopped working for us years ago."

"Thought it was broke, but we held onto it just in case," Tock added. "Now we're realizing that it should be yours."

"But I don't think I'll remember all those instructions." I said.

"Nothing to it, really." Tick said. "Just wind it up every day, and the rest will take care of itself."

"Just don't forget to record your adventures when the watch does its thing," Pappy said. "Then come back and share 'em with us."

"But, you haven't even told me what it does. How will I know if it works?" I asked.

"Oh, you'll know." They all grinned.

6. Y-u-M-S

I wore my new watch to bed that night, and the next morning it fit me perfectly, just like Tick said it would. I was so excited I ran to the kitchen to tell Mom and Dad.

When I got there, Dad was sitting at the table reading his dumb grown-up newspaper and drinking his smelly coffee. Before I could show him the watch, he started talking.

"Your mother tells me the school called

yesterday," he said. He did this thing, which he does a lot, where he didn't even look up from his newspaper, just like Val with her phone. It's really rude. I know it's rude 'cause every time I don't look at Mom and Dad, they tell me how rude I'm being. But I guess it's okay to be rude if you're a grown-up reading the newspaper.

I didn't say anything back 'cause what Dad said wasn't even a question, but I guess Dad thought it was. He looked at me and said, "Well, Winston, what do you have to say for yourself?"

I didn't have anything to say about Ms. Perkles calling, so it seemed like a good time to tell him about the watch instead. "Dad, you're not going to believe this. I got a new—well, actually, I guess it's old, but it—"

"Winston, do not derail this conversation. We've been through this a hundred times: you cannot argue with Ms. Perkles about how to spell Williams."

"You're wrong!" I told Dad. "It hasn't been a

hundred times—only four times. You're using hyper-bullies."

Dad doesn't like it when I correct him, but since he's the one that taught me about hyper-bullies, I figured it was okay. Plus, Ms. Perkles said I'm really good with my numbers, so I knew four times was the right number.

"It's hyperboles, Winston, not hyper-bullies . . . but I am not going to have this conversation with you right now." Then he confused me, 'cause even though he told me he wasn't going to have the conversation, he just kept right on talking. "You know we don't spell our name with a Y-U-M-S."

"But that's how you spell yums!"

"Look, son, I am your father, not your foe. Life will be easier if you learn that since I'm a grown-up, I know what's best."

"What's a foe?" I asked.

"A foe is someone that acts with or expresses enmity toward another person."

"Someone who what?"

Dad had to think really hard and then he finally said, "A foe is like an enemy—someone who's against you—and I'm not your foe." For someone that knows a lot of big words, he sure has a hard time using normal ones.

"So . . . a foe is like a super-villain?"

"Sure. Yeah, like a villain. The point is I am *not* your foe. I'm your dad and a grown-up, and I know what's best. I just want you to grow up, be more mature, and stop acting like such a child all the time. Do we have a deal?"

A deal? I had no idea what he was talking about. Why did he want me to stop acting like a child? I am a child. Why would I want to be a grown-up? Grown-ups have no fun, and having no fun is something a villain would want me to do.

Of course, I knew if I told Dad there was no deal, he would just try harder to make me boring, so I just nodded. "Deal."

"Great." Dad smiled. "By the way, is that a new watch?" He pulled my arm toward his face.

"Yeah, Tick and Tock gave it to me," I said.

He squinted, tapped the watch a few times, and shrugged. "Maybe next time they'll give you a watch that works."

That's when I remembered I still needed to wind it up for the day, which I did right away, so I could show Dad it wasn't broken. The numbers moved to the right place and hands started spinning like crazy, until the short hand pointed to the 8 and the long hand to the 12.

Before I could show Dad that it was working, he was already walking out the front door to his dumb job. He popped his head back in and said, "Winston, I mean it: no more calls, otherwise, you won't touch your video games for a year."

*****

During school, Ms. Perkles didn't leave me alone—especially when she handed out the math worksheet. She hovered over just like she did the day before and watched me write my name.

W-i-n-s-t-o-n W-i-l-l- . . .

I looked up at Ms. Perkles, and she gave me a funny look. I knew she wanted me to spell my name her way—the wrong way. I didn't want to lose video games, so I almost did what she wanted. But at the last second, I remembered how Mom and Dad always say to do the right thing, even when it is really hard. That's how come I decided to write my name the way I know it should be spelled.

W-i-l-l-y-u-m-s

As soon as I finished, Ms. Perkles took a deep breath through her nostrils ('cause her lips were pinched shut) before she finally said something. "Winston, I don't even know what to say right now. It's like you are incapable of learning simple things."

"Maybe you're incapable of learning simple things!" I said back. I don't know what *incapable* means, but if Ms. Perkles was allowed to say it to me, I guessed it was okay for me to say it to her. I guessed wrong.

"In all my years"—Ms. Perkles put her hand over her heart and acted all shocked—"I have never had a student be so belligerent toward me."

"Belligerent? What does that mean?"

"It means you are beyond rude. You're treating me like I am your enemy, but I am only trying to help. When will you understand that I am a grown-up and know best?"

When she mentioned enemies and knowing what was best, I remembered what Dad said about foes. I spelled my name the right way, but all the grown-ups were trying to stop me. In my comic books, villains are always trying to stop the superheroes from doing the right thing. Was Ms. Perkles a villain? Was she my foe?

If she was, someone had to stand up to her, so I climbed up on my chair and then onto my desk. Out of nowhere, words popped into my head, and I blurted them out.

"Don't be my foe! Time to know what I know!"

You'll probably think I am making this up, but the next part is all true.

The hands on the watch started spinning like crazy, and the numbers tumbled around like they were in a washing machine. The watch started floating up and pulled my arm high in the air, until I looked like a superhero about to fly away.

Then this super weird wave of bright light shot out from the watch in a big circle, like when you throw a rock in the water, and it makes all those circles that start small but get bigger and bigger. There was also a bunch of sparks and flashes, like fireworks.

"Whoa! Did you see that?" I asked, but I guess no one did. Everyone acted like nothing had happened. All the other kids just kept working on their math, like they couldn't wait to be lame grown-ups.

At first, Ms. Perkles didn't say anything, either. She just stared at me with a weird look. I thought maybe I'd made her super, super mad, 'cause I'd never seen that look before, but it turns out she wasn't mad.

She put her hand over her mouth and started talking to herself. "Oh my. What have I done?"

"Are you talking about the watch?" I asked.

"What watch?" Ms. Perkles looked at my wrist and then shook her head like she just realized I was wearing the watch. "Winston, it's a very lovely watch, but I was talking about how terribly, horribly, tremendously awful I have been to you and how very, very, very wrong I've been. Will you forgive me?"

At first, I didn't know what to say. Ms. Perkles was acting weird. "Uh . . . sure," I finally said. I was confused, 'cause she had never apologized to me—for anything—ever. "What for?" I asked, thinking this might be some kind of trick.

"Why, spelling your name wrong. You've been right this whole time, which makes me wrong. We've all been wrong!"

"Are you playing a joke on me?"

Val, my cousin, sometimes acts like she believes what I'm saying, and then she'll roll her eyes and tell me I'm just a dumb little kid that no one actually believes, and that she was only pretending to believe me as a joke, which I don't get, 'cause there's no punchline, and Pappy says every good joke has a good punchline.

"Goodness, no!" She took my hand and helped me down from the desk. "Come with me."

Ms. Perkles pulled me out of the classroom and down the hall. It didn't take me long to figure out where we were headed.

"The principal!" I said. "You're taking me to the principal? So, it is a joke. Well, it's not a funny one."

I was thinking about how the principal said he would

call Mom and Dad if I got sent to his office again and how Dad said I'd lose video games if that happened.

Ms. Perkles stopped walking, got down on her knees, and hugged me. If this was a joke, it got more confusing and weirder every minute.

"Winston, I promise this is not a joke. I'm going to make everything right again." She looked like she was about to cry. "I'm so sorry."

When we got to the principal's office, Mrs. Butters told Ms. Perkles that the principal was busy. Ms. Perkles told Mrs. Butters that this was more important. Mrs. Butters looked at me, then back at Ms. Perkles, and agreed.

The next thing I know, I'm sitting in Mr. L's office and Ms. Perkles is telling him all about her mistake. "Winston was right—always has been. *Y-U-M-S*. How did I not see it? It is how you make a *yums* sound." That last part she said like she was talking to herself. Then she cried. "Winston tried to explain, but I didn't listen. I'm sooooooo sorry. He never should've been sent to your office."

Mr. L's face went white. He pulled out my school file and started flipping through the pages. "Oh no. How could this happen?" He looked at Ms. Perkles and then at me. "I was wrong, as well, but it looks like we weren't the only two." He held up a piece of paper with Mom's writing on it. "Even his parents spell it wrong. We've *all* been wrong."

Ms. Perkles put her arm around me. "Don't worry, Winston; we are going to fix this."

Mr. L picked up the phone and told the person

on the other end to come to the school *immediately* and that it was an *emergency*. When he hung up, he told me Mom and Dad were on their way.

"What? You called Mom and Dad?" I was glad people were finally listening, but Dad specifically said he didn't want any more calls, and I did not want to lose video games.

To my surprise, things got even weirder when Mom and Dad got there. They weren't mad at all. After Ms. Perkles and Mr. L told them what happened, Mom and Dad hugged me and told me how sorry they were. Everybody was saying sorry a lot. Luckily, Dad didn't say anything about video games.

"This is so embarrassing," Dad said. "I'm a lawyer who has spelled his name wrong on every legal document I've ever signed. I'm going to call Judge Jackson and get this fixed right away—I'm calling in every favor anyone owes me to correct this mistake immediately."

Dad got out his cell phone and started dialing a bunch of numbers. Then we all went down to the courthouse, and Dad met with the judge. They signed a ton of papers. Then Judge Jackson told us, "It's official: your name has been legally corrected from Williams to Will*yums*."

Mom and Dad spent the rest of the day on their phones and computers changing all their bank accounts, ordering new business cards, and hiring people to change the signs at Dad's work. They were so busy fixing everything that I had to put myself to bed.

****

The next morning, I overheard Mom and Dad talking. They didn't know I was listening.

"I don't understand what came over us," Dad said.

"I wish I knew," said Mom. "It was the strangest thing. Why did we think Winston was right?"

"More important, how are we going to re-fix

this?" Dad pinched the top of his nose, which he does sometimes when he's stressed. "Why did I change everything to Will*yums*." He raised his voice when he said the *yums* part.

"Can't we just change everything back?" Mom asked.

"It's already embarrassing enough that we changed it in the first place. If I change it back, people will think I've lost my mind, and no one wants that kind of lawyer. Besides, I called in every favor. I'm all out."

"We can't leave it, can we?"

Dad took a deep breath and rubbed his eyes. He nodded. "I don't like it, but I see no other choice."

Mom sighed. "I guess it's time to accept that we are now Susan and Henry Will*yums*." She raised her voice at the *yums* part, just like Dad.

"There is one silver lining," he said.

"What's that?"

"Won't be getting any more calls from the school

about Winston misspelling his name."

Mom smiled, then Dad did too. Then they both started laughing, but I don't know why, 'cause what Dad said wasn't even funny.

7. FrANkLiN SaYs SoRry

I spent all day trying to remember the magic phrase, but I couldn't. All I remembered was that it was something about foes. I tried a bunch of things, but nothing worked.

I even lifted my arm in the air like a superhero, but Ms. Perkles just thought I was raising my hand to ask a question. When I told her that I was trying to get my watch to work, she sighed and told me I shouldn't be so disruptive. I raised my hand to ask what *disruptive* meant, but she ignored me.

At lunch, I sat next to Max. Max's mom always packs good stuff in his lunch, like chips and fruit snacks and pudding. My mom doesn't pack any of those things. Usually, I only get a peanut butter and jelly sandwich and something healthy like carrots, which I don't like at all, or celery, which I only eat if I'm starving.

I once told Mom about Max's lunches and that she should pack the same stuff for me. She didn't agree. Instead, she told me that if she did, I would probably turn into an *entitled brat*, which she said is a kid who gets everything they want without working for it. I didn't tell Mom, 'cause she said it like it was a bad thing, but being an entitled brat sounded awesome.

Anyway, at lunch, Max had pudding and leftover pizza. I offered him carrots, but he wouldn't trade, so I put my arm in the air and said, "You're being a foe. Now give me your pudding." Nothing happened, except that Max grabbed his pudding and held it close to him, like I was gonna steal it or something.

"Heck no," he said. "You're acting weird."

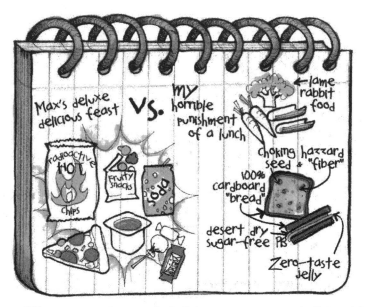

"I'm not acting weird. It's my new watch," I told him.

"Your watch is acting weird?" Max asked, but he said it like he thought I was crazy.

"No. Try to comprehend what I'm saying." That's something Dad says to me a lot when I'm not understanding him. "Yesterday this watch was working, but today it's not."

"Looks like it's working," Max said after he grabbed my arm and looked at the watch. "But it's just a dumb watch, so it only tells time."

"It's not dumb!"

"It is too! I have a smart watch that does cool stuff. Yours doesn't, which makes it a dumb watch."

Max's *smart* watch works like a tiny phone. Mom says there's no reason for a child my age to have a smart watch, but I disagree. A smart watch tells time, the weather, sends text messages, says how fast your heart is beating, and probably a million other things. So actually, there's a million reasons to have a smart watch.

"It's not a dumb watch," I told Max. "You're dumb."

He didn't talk to me for the rest of the day, but I didn't mind. Making my watch work was way more important.

I was still trying to make it work while walking home from school. I tapped the cover a bunch. I wound it up again. I shook my arm super fast. I ran and punched the sky. I was so distracted, I didn't pay attention to where I was going. Out of nowhere, I ran right into someone who was bad news: Franklin.

"Watch where you're going, Whiny-baby-ston," he said. "You look like a doofus!"

I wished my watch hadn't distracted me from remembering to look out for him.

"Leave me alone," I told him. "I have really important things to do today."

"Like what—be stupid? 'Cause you're already a master at being stupid."

"I'm not stupid!" I yelled. "Also, you're not supposed to say *stupid*."

Franklin did a fake punch, where he pretended he was gonna hit me but only punched halfway. I flinched.

"What's-a matter, Whiny-baby-ston? You scared?"

"I'm not scared!" But I was mad—mad at my body for flinching and making me look scared.

"Then why'd you flinch?" Franklin did another fake punch, and I flinched again, even though I tried not to. "You're such a scared baby."

"I'm not scared of you, and I'm not a baby!"

"Oh, is Whiny-baby-ston gonna cry?"

"Stop! You don't know anything! You're the one who's scared."

Franklin grabbed me by the shirt with both hands and pulled me toward him. "I know everything, and you know nothing. I'll never be scared of a wimpy, little baby like you. You couldn't scare a tiny bunny."

"Not true! I am scary! All I have to do is look at you and you'll be so scared you'll cry AND pee your pants."

Franklin laughed—not a laugh like when you hear a funny joke but one like he was making fun of me, like a bully. "That's what you said last time, but you're no hero."

Him saying *hero* made me think of villains and foes, and out of nowhere, the words I had been trying to remember all day popped right into my head again. I yelled them.

"Don't be my foe! Time to know what I know!"

That's when it happened again. The dials on my watch started spinning like crazy, the numbers tumbled around, and the watch pulled my arm high in the air. Then a ripple wave of light shot out from the watch in every direction, with a bunch of sparks and flashes.

Franklin made a face like he just remembered something. He let go of my shirt and made a scared face. Then he made a surprised face, then an embarrassed face. He looked down.

There was a big wet spot on the crotch of his pants; it got bigger and moved down his legs. Franklin started crying, just like a little baby.

"You just peed your pants!" I tried not to laugh, but I couldn't help it.

"It's—not—my—fault." Franklin made big sniffles and cries between every word.

"It is your fault, 'cause you're a bully and you didn't believe me."

"I'm so sorry." Franklin was still sniffling

"If you're mean again, I'm gonna tell everyone— especially the girls—that you peed your pants."

"I'll never be mean again." Franklin ran into his house, still crying.

8. Master Chef

The next morning, Mom gave me the worst news ever.

"They need me in the office fulltime." She said the next part like it was no big deal, but it was a huge deal—the hugest! "Val is going to babysit you every day for the next few weeks."

"No!" I yelled. "She's the worst! I'd rather be sent to an orphanage!"

"Winston, please. I don't have time to argue with

you, and I certainly don't have time for your overreacting."

"I'm not overreacting—I'm underreacting! Val is the worst babysitter ever! You can't do this to me! I'll call the cops on you!"

"Winston, the decision is final." Mom looked at her watch and then said one of the words I'm not allowed to say. "I can't talk anymore, or I'm going to be late."

Seeing Mom look at her watch reminded me that my watch was still in my room. I ran as fast as I could, grabbed it, wound it up, slapped it on my wrist, and ran back to Mom. Just before she walked out the door I yelled, "Mom, you're a foe! Now, don't let Val babysit me."

Nothing happened.

*****

Paying attention at school was really hard. I was too mad about Val babysitting *every* day. A starving lion who ate kids could do a better job babysitting.

When the bell rang at the end of the day, using my watch was the only idea I had for fixing the Val problem, but I'd forgotten the magic phrase, again. There was nothing I could do.

When I got home, Val was sitting on the couch, playing on her phone, like usual. She didn't look up or anything, but I didn't care, 'cause she was watching one of my favorite shows: *Outdoor Ozzie*.

It's about this guy named Ozzie. He gets lost in the wilderness on purpose and teaches you to survive without any help. This time, Ozzie was lost in the mountains. He was surviving by eating plant roots. Some of them, he said, tasted almost like potatoes.

"I could survive in the wilderness, just like Ozzie," I told Val.

"Ehh . . . doubtful. Eating your own boogers doesn't make you a survival expert." Val laughed as if what she said was funny, but it wasn't. "So, let me tell you the same thing I told you last time: shut it!"

"That's not what you told me," I told her. "You said for me to shut my face, which you didn't know was impossible."

"Whatever."

"Also, I know way more about survival than you do. The only thing you know how to do is play on your cell phone and be a big meanie."

"Well, how's this for being a meanie?" She turned off the TV. "No more TV for the booger-eating know-it-all."

I gave Val the meanest look I could. Without TV, I started noticing how empty my stomach was. "I'm hungry," I said.

"Don't care," Val said.

"But you're the babysitter! Your job is to take care of me."

Val put down her phone looking all frustrated. "Quit bothering me!"

"Fine. I'll make my own snack."

"Nope—you're not allowed in the kitchen. Your

mom gave me strict directions to keep you out."

"That's a lie. Mom would never do that."

"Maybe you forgot about the last time. I don't think your mom wants anymore baseball bat stew from her *master chef* son."

"So, you think I'm a master chef?"

"It's called sarcasm." She went back to her phone and not looking at me, but I could tell she was rolling her eyes. I'd get in trouble for doing that, but Val never gets in trouble for anything. It's so unfair.

Before I could say anything else, Val said, "As evidenced by the dumb look on your face, you obviously don't know what *sarcasm* is. It's when you say something but actually mean the opposite."

"So, you're saying I'm the opposite of a master chef?"

"Bingo. Can't get anything past you, *genius*." Then she said, "That's me being sarcastic again, just in case you thought I was actually calling you a genius."

Val was making me so mad, I decided to be

sarcastic, too. "Well, I think you're a good babysitter."

"Oh, thank you. That is so sweet of you to say," Val said all nice, as if I was being serious, which I wasn't.

"I was being sarcastic," I said, biting down on my teeth really tight 'cause of how mad I was getting.

"Didn't sound like it." Val looked up from her phone finally. "Now, if you don't mind, I've got more important things to do, so why don't you get lost?"

What could be more important for a babysitter than babysitting?

"No!" I told her. "I'm not getting lost until you admit that I'm a master chef and you are a bad babysitter—and no being sarcastic when you say it!"

Val laughed. "Tell you what: if you can make a dinner that your mom and dad actually like, I'll tell your parents I'm a horrible babysitter and that they should pay you to babysit me. But that'll never happen, especially when your banned from the kitchen."

I started to think that she might be right. The kitchen is where all the pots and food and spices are. Then I thought about *Outdoor Ozzie*. I didn't need a kitchen. I just needed to think like a survival expert.

I went outside and found an old bucket; it was a little dirty, but that was no problem. I just wiped most of the dirt off with my sleeve. Then I started adding ingredients.

Ozzie always says the first step to survival is finding a *natural water source*. Luckily, there was plenty of water in the bird bath. I chased the birds away and scooped the water into the bucket with my hands.

Since I didn't have any potatoes, I pulled up a bunch of weeds. The roots were smaller, but they looked a lot like the ones on *Outdoor Ozzie*, which he said tasted like potatoes, so I threw them in the bucket.

Finding chicken was tougher 'cause we don't keep any chicken outside—only in the kitchen. I thought and thought and thought, but I couldn't think of any good answers. I started to worry I'd have to make soup without chicken when I heard Mr. Price's dog, Baxter, start barking, which gave me an idea.

Mr. Price is our neighbor, and one time he told me that he will only feed Baxter food that is made with real chicken. Luckily for me, Baxter is what Mr. Price calls an *outdoor dog*, so Baxter's dog food bowl is also kept outside.

I hopped the fence to Mr. Price's yard and found Baxter's food bowl on the back porch. I was expecting it to look more like chicken nuggets, but it looked just like regular dog food. I scooped up a big handful, plopped it into my bucket, and mixed it with the water.

Baxter growled at me like I was stealing. I promised to bring him some chicken nuggets as

soon as I was allowed in the kitchen again, which made it more like borrowing, not stealing.

I thought spices were gonna be the trickiest part, but they weren't. They were the easiest. I remembered that on the cooking show, the chef used some spices that looked like chopped up leaves. There were tons of leaves in our backyard.

I was ripping up big handfuls of leaves and throwing them in the bucket when I saw Mom and Dad driving up the street. There was no time for taste tests. I ran inside and set the table as fast as I could. I finished just as Mom and Dad walked in.

"Not again." Mom shook her head and frowned when she saw dinner on the table.

"Mom, just try it. It is the best soup ever."

"I doubt that." Dad poked at it with his spoon. "It smells like soggy dog food."

"That's the real chicken," I said. "Now trust me, it's the best soup ever."

Val leaned over and whispered in my ear, "Looks like it's time for you to admit defeat." She sounded just like a villain from one of my comic books.

I was about to tell her I would never admit defeat, just like the hero would say, but those were not the words that came out.

"Don't be my foe! Time to know what I know!"

The watch dials went crazy and the numbers tumbled around. My hand lifted, and the sparking ripple wave of light blasted through the air. The next thing I knew, Mom, Dad, *and* Val were all scarfing down my soup. When their bowls were empty, they filled 'em back up and kept eating until the bucket was empty.

They chomped down every last root, devoured all of the Baxter's chicken dog food, swallowed every leaf, and slurped down every drop before I even got to try it.

"Oh, Winston, you were right." Mom leaned back in her chair with her hand on her belly. "That was the best soup I've ever had."

Dad nodded in agreement.

I smiled at Val. "Did you hear that? I think you have something you need to tell them."

"Gladly." Val stood up. I thought she would be mad, but she looked really happy and said, "Uncle Henry, Aunt Susan, Winston is a master chef, and I'm a horrible babysitter—the worst! You should pay Winston to babysit me!"

9. ESCAPE

On Saturday, I finally got to go see Pappy, Tick, and Tock. When I got done telling 'em about Mom and Dad fixing our last name, Franklin peeing his pants, and Val admitting that she was the worst, Pappy jumped out of his seat and skipped around, cheering. He hugged me, lifting me off the ground.

"It works—the watch still works!" Tick and Tock were jumping for joy, too.

"Well, it only sorta works," I confessed.

"Whatdya mean?" Tock raised his eyebrows.

"Well . . . it doesn't always work when I want it to, 'cause I keep forgetting the magic phrase. So, it only sorta works."

Tick and Tock both laughed. "Sounds like it works just the way it always has," Tick said. "Part of the watch's magic is making you forget the phrase until it is most important to remember."

"Doesn't grant wishes," Tock shook his head, "but it'll always work when you truly need it to."

"If it did grant wishes, I'd wish for all my books back," Pappy said.

"And our clocks," Tick said.

"What do you mean?" I asked.

"Rotten Mr. Norman took our treasures for real this time. He locked 'em up in his office," Pappy said.

I looked under their beds: no books, no clocks.

"All our precious treasures! He even took the clocks off our shelves because *any clock that nearly pokes out an eye is a safety hazard.*" Tock imitated Mr. Norman's whiny voice when he said the last part.

"But Winston, you should see him now." Pappy started laughing so hard he could barely say the next part. "Ever since he got jabbed in the eye by Tick's cuckoo clock, he's been wearing an eye patch. He looks just like a real, true blue, evil pirate."

We all laughed, but I was still mad about what Mr. Norman did. He was like a grown-up version of Franklin. "Isn't that stealing? He can't do that," I said. "Can he?"

"Not much we can do about it. We're just a few old geezers that no one listens to," Pappy said. "Everyone else thinks they know what's best for us."

I knew how they felt. "I'll tell Dad," I said. "He's a lawyer—he can take Mr. Norman to court and they'll throw him in jail if he doesn't give your stuff back."

Pappy shook his head. "I already called Henry. He took Mr. Norman's side. Anyhow, even if we got our stuff back, Mr. Norman will never let us keep it under the beds again."

"Yeah," Tock said. "We'd have to escape to a place where people like Mr. Norman and Henry can't find us."

"Well, there's gotta be something we can do," I said. I thought about Franklin and how he peed his pants.

I could make Mr. Norman pee his pants, I thought. I smiled when I pictured it, but I wasn't sure how that would help get their treasures back or help them escape.

"We'll just have to accept that the rest of our existence will be here, at the hands of an evil pirate, without our treasures," Pappy said.

That's when an idea hit me. "I know how to stop him!" I shouted. "Mr. Norman is an evil pirate, right? We just have to figure out who can stop an evil pirate."

"As far as I know," Pappy frowned, "no one can

stop pirates. Storybooks are full of kings and queens who have tried, but it's always the pirates who are escaping."

"That's it!" I shouted. "Good Pirates! All we need is good pirates—then you can get your stuff back and escape!" I started jumping with excitement.

"Slow down, boy. Where are we going to find good pirates?"

"Right here!" I yelled, but Pappy, Tick, and Tock just looked back and forth at each other, all confused. I waited for them to understand what I was saying, but they just weren't getting it. "We're the good pirates! We'll get your treasure back and escape."

They all frowned. Pappy put his arm around me. "Winston, it means the world that you want to help, but this is just the reality of getting old—grown-up problems. Pretending to be pirates, as much as I wish it did, is not going to help."

Pappy had never acted like this before. He

sounded like Ms. Perkles and Mom and Dad—a boring grown-up. For the first time ever, he didn't believe in me. Even Tick and Tock looked at me like they thought my idea wasn't going to work.

I stomped my foot. "You're wrong! I'm a good pirate, and you're good pirates. We're the bravest pirates ever. We're the only ones who can make evil Captain Norman walk the plank!" I raised my watch in the air and the words came.

"Arrr! Don't be my foe! Time to know what I know!"

Dials spun, numbers tumbled, and the waves and sparks shot out from the watch. Everything changed.

Pappy scrunched his face up. "Aye, aye, Cap'n. But we be needing a ship. I saw me some abandoned sails over yonder, free fer the taking." He pointed out the door.

I ran out into the hall where I found a big laundry

cart on wheels—the perfect ship—big enough for all of us. When I came back with the pirate ship, Pappy, Tick, and Tock were all wearing pirate hats made from newspaper. Pappy had an extra one for me. It was a little big, but I still liked it.

Tock held out his cane. It was wrapped in foil, so it looked like it was metal. "Your cutlass, Cap'n Winston." Tick and Tock both bowed their heads as I took it.

"A *cutlass*?" I'd never heard that word before.

"It be pirate for sword," Tock whispered as he handed me an eye patch made from a plastic spoon tied to a string.

"Arrr, avast ye; we be on a quest to get back our booty from the evil scallywag, Big Belly Norman, cap'n of the geezer ship. A brave cap'n be what we need." Pappy had one eye squashed shut and his lip was raised on one side, so his mouth looked crooked. "Yer the only cap'n we trust."

His pirate voice was better than mine, but I did

my best. "Arrr, we'll make him walk the plank!"

"Yo-ho!" Tick and Tock both yelled together. Tick stood up. "Arrr, the salty hag hornswoggled us and stole away our timepieces and adventure books! Word on the sea be that he locked the treasure away in his hideout."

"Lead the way, Cap'n Winston!" Tock shouted.

"Weigh anchor and hoist the mizzen! Time to reclaim our booty!" Pappy called out. "Off we be to that ol' seadog's hideout, and then we escape this prison once and for all!"

They all cheered and climbed into the pirate ship, and I pushed them down the ocean hallway to Captain Norman's office hideout. I busted through the door and found the rotten scoundrel counting all his plundered treasures, eye patch and all.

"You?" He looked up at me. "What want ye?"

"Arrrgg, I think ye know what I wants." I gave him the cruelest look I could and held up my cutlass. "Ye stole treasure from me mates. We be here to take back what be theirs and make ye walk the plank."

Captain Norman jumped out of his chair, grabbed his umbrella cutlass and then climbed up on his desk. "I took treasure from no one. That there booty be nothing but junk." He pointed to the corner of his hideout, where there were several stacked boxes overflowing with books and clocks. Sitting on top was the donkey clock and the clock that poked Mr. Norman in the eye. On the outside of the boxes, in black marker, was written *Trash*.

"Ye fiend!" I ran for the boxes.

"Arr. I'll see it buried at sea and ye can't stop me!" Captain Norman jumped down and blocked my path; then he swung his cutlass at me. "En garde!"

I blocked his swing, and our sword fight started. Pappy, Tick, and Tock all cheered until Captain Norman knocked the cutlass from my hand and kicked it behind him, toward the boxes.

"Any last words before I make ye shark bait?" He held his cutlass high over his head, ready to strike.

I grinned. "Look behind ye."

Captain Norman turned to look. "There's nothing behi—"

As he was turning, I dove between his legs and grabbed my cutlass. Before he could do anything, I knocked the blade from his hand. He dropped to his knees and begged for his life.

"Ye can live, but ye must pay fer ye crimes," I said with a grin.

Pappy, Tick, Tock, and I marched Captain

Norman to the pool. I poked him with my cutlass until he stepped out to the edge of the diving board plank.

"For yer crimes of hornswoggling and plundering booty that be not yers, I sentence ye to walk the plank." I gave him a soft poke with my cutlass, and he splashed into the water below.

We sailed back to Captain Norman's hideout, loaded all of Pappy's books and Tick and Tock's clocks aboard our ship, and sailed out the automatic doors.

That's when I realized how late it was. I told Pappy, Tick, and Tock that I needed to get home for dinner and asked if they were coming with me.

"'Fraid not, Cap'n," Tock said. "Now that we've reclaimed our booty, Big Belly Norman will come fer us, soon as he swims ashore."

"No doubt he'll make a pirate's oath with his ally, the Dull Pirate Henry," said Pappy. "They'll take to the high seas until they capture us and lock us away, back in Cap'n Norman's prison for geezer pirates. 'Fraid we must find a secret hideout of our own."

"Arrr, 'tis true, 'tis true." Tick cheered. "But we shall send fer ya, our fearless cap'n, when the time be right."

"Yer secret be safe with me," I told them.

As they sailed off, Tock yelled, "If ye want to find us, follow the chimes of the clock to the place lesser heroes dare not go."

I wasn't sure what that meant, but I decided I would do my best to remember that hint.

*****

The next morning, Mr. Norman called Dad during breakfast. I thought I was busted for sure, but I was wrong. When Dad hung up the phone, he looked confused and worried. Then he chuckled a single chuckle—not a that's-so-funny chuckle but more like a that's-strange-but-I'm-still-a-boring-grown-up chuckle.

"What was that all about?" Mom asked.

Dad shook his head. "Apparently, Pappy and his roommates stole stuff from Mr. Norman's office yesterday and fled the scene. No one has seen them since."

"Oh dear. That hardly seems a laughing matter." Mom put her hand over her mouth. "How did three men as old as them ever do such a thing?"

"That's the strange part." Dad chuckled again. "Mr. Norman claims a pirate helped them."

"A pirate?" Mom gasped.

"Yep." Dad shook his head again while grinning. "He claims a mysterious pirate captain with a sword showed up, broke into his office, stole several boxes of books and clocks, and forced him to walk the plank. He said that even though the pirate was the size of a child, he was the scariest man he'd ever encountered."

I smiled. "It's actually called a cutlass."

"What?" Dad was looking at me like I was an alien or something.

"You called it a sword, but a pirate sword is called a cutlass."

"My, don't you know a lot about pirates." Mom looked really impressed with my pirate knowledge. Then she said, "Maybe you're the mysterious pirate Mr. Norman is so afraid of."

I froze, but then Mom and Dad both laughed like it was the funniest, craziest thing they'd ever heard. After a little while I smiled. Mom and Dad probably thought I was smiling at Mom's joke, but I wasn't.

I was smiling because I knew that Pappy, Tick, and Tock, were finally happy in their new hideout— and I was going to find them.

This is Lee Gangles. He had tons of adventures when he was little, but I guess he forgot about them 'cause one day he turned into a lame, boring grown-up. (The worst, most boring kind — a lawyer).

Luckily, his awesome **not** boring kids started making him take them on adventures every night, before bed. When he finally remembered that adventures are awesome, he quit being lame. Now his favorite thing to do is read and write adventure logs, like this one!

This is Christy C. Robinson.
She has been drawing since she
first wrapped her sturdy baby fist
around a crayon – like a million
years ago. She illustrated her
first published book when she was
my cousin Val's age. She's had lots
of artsy fartsy jobs since then.

For fun she likes to draw while
traveling with her husband
and their 3 kids.
She also likes to draw
with her kids and
sometimes even
draws ON them!

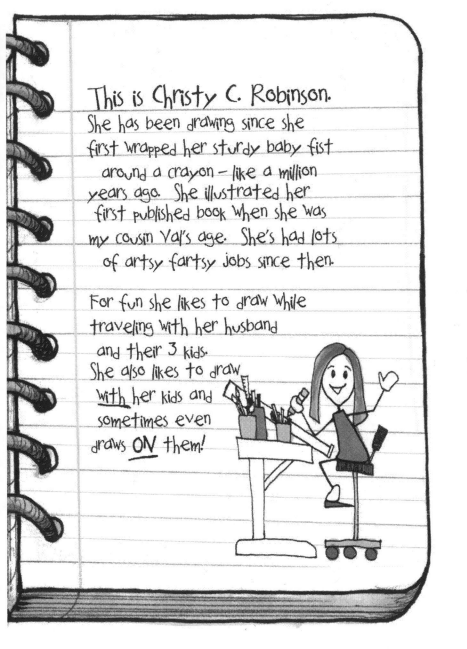

Be sure to check out this other awesome book by Lee Gangles:

Made in the USA
Middletown, DE
09 February 2021

33473535R00073